A MICHAEL NEUGEBAUER BOOK
Copyright © 1988 Neugebauer Press, Salzburg, Austria.
Original title: "Tischlein Deck Dich, Goldesel und Knüppel aus dem Sack."
Published and distributed in USA by PICTURE BOOK STUDIO Ltd., Saxonville, MA.
Distributed in Canada by Vanwell Publishing, St. Catharines.
Published in UK by PICTURE BOOK STUDIO, Neugebauer Press Ltd., London.
Distributed in UK by Ragged Bears, Andover.
Distributed in Australia by Era Publications, Adelaide.
All rights reserved.
Printed in Austria

LIBRARY OF CONGRESS CATALOGING IN PUBLICATION DATA
The wishing table / by the Brothers Grimm: illustrated by Eve Tharlet.
Translation of: Tischlein deck dich, Goldesel Knüppel aus dem Sack.
Summary: Three brothers who leave home because of a greedy goat,
return to share with their father the magic rewards of their hard work.
ISBN 0-88708-064-2
[1. Fairy tales. 2. Folklore--Germany.] I. Grimm, Jacob, 1785-1863.
II. Grimm, Wilhelm, 1786-1859. III. Tharlet, Eve, ill. IV. Title.
PZ8.I.W765   1988
398.2'1'0943--dc19   87-32664

Ask your bookseller for these other PICTURE BOOK STUDIO books
illustrated by Eve Tharlet:
THE PRINCESS AND THE PEA by H.C. Andersen
DIZZY FROM FOOLS by M.L. Miller
And these others by The Brothers Grimm:
LITTLE RED CAP illustrated by Lisbeth Zwerger
HANSEL AND GRETEL illustrated by Lisbeth Zwerger
THE SEVEN RAVENS illustrated by Lisbeth Zwerger
SNOW WHITE AND THE SEVEN DWARVES illustrated by Chihiro Iwasaki

The Brothers Grimm

THE WISHING TABLE

illustrated by Eve Tharlet · translated by Anthea Bell

PICTURE BOOK STUDIO

Once upon a time there was a tailor who had three sons and just one goat. Now as the goat fed them all with her milk, she needed good food, and she was put out to graze every day. The tailor's three sons took turns taking her out. One day the eldest son took her to the churchyard, where the finest plants grew, and let her graze and frolic about there. In the evening, when it was time to go home, he asked, "Goat, have you had enough to eat?"

And the goat replied: "I'm full up to the teeth.

Couldn't eat another leaf.

Ble-ea-eat! Ble-ea-eat!"

"Come along home, then," said the boy, and he took her by the halter, led her home to her shed and tied her up.

"Well," said the old tailor, "has the goat had plenty to eat?"

"Oh yes," said his son. "She's full up to the teeth, and couldn't eat another leaf." However, the father wanted to make sure of that for himself, so he went down to the stable, stroked his beloved goat and asked, "Goat, are you sure you've had enough to eat?"

And the goat replied: "Where would I get enough to eat?

I've been jumping over stony ground,

where there wasn't a blade of grass to be found.

Ble-ea-eat! Ble-ea-eat!"

"What's all this?" cried the tailor, and he went up to the house and said to the boy, "Why, you liar, how dare you say the goat's had enough to eat when you let her go hungry?" And in his fury he took his yardstick down from the wall and chased his son out of the house with it.

Next day it was the second son's turn. He chose a place near the garden hedge where plenty of good plants grew, and the goat ate them all.

In the evening, when he was about to go home,
he asked, "Goat, have you had enough to eat?"
And the goat replied: "I'm full up to the teeth.
          Couldn't eat another leaf.
          Ble-ea-eat! Ble-ea-eat!"
"Come along home, then," said the boy, and he took her home and tied her up in the shed.
"Well," said the old tailor, "has the goat had plenty to eat?"
"Oh yes," said his son. "She's full up to the teeth, and couldn't eat another leaf."

But the tailor wasn't going to take his son's word for it, so he went down to the shed and asked, "Goat, are you sure you've had enough to eat?"

And the goat replied: "Where would I get enough to eat?

I've been jumping over stony ground,

where there wasn't a blade of grass to be found.

Ble-ea-eat! Ble-ea-eat!"

"Oh, the wicked rascal!" cried the tailor. "Letting a good goat like you go hungry!"

And he went up and chased the boy out of doors with his yardstick.

Now it was the third son's turn. He wanted to make a good job of it, so he looked for bushes with the very best leaves and let the goat eat them. In the evening, when he was about to go home, he asked, "Goat, have you had enough to eat?"

And the goat replied: "I'm full up to the teeth.

Couldn't eat another leaf.

Ble-ea-eat! Ble-ea-eat!"

"Come along home, then," said the boy, and he led her back to her shed and tied her up.

"Well," said the old tailor, "has the goat had plenty to eat?"

Oh yes," said his son. "She's full up to the teeth, and couldn't eat another leaf."

But the tailor wasn't so sure of that, so he went down and asked, "Goat, are you sure you've had enough to eat?"

And the naughty goat replied:

"Where would I get enough to eat?

I've been jumping over stony ground,

where there wasn't a blade of grass to be found.

Ble-ea-eat! Ble-ea-eat!"

"Oh, what a set of liars!" cried the tailor. "Every one of them as wicked and undutiful as his brothers. Well, you won't fool me any longer!" And quite beside himself with rage, he hurried back up and thrashed the poor boy so hard with his yardstick that he ran out of the house.

So now the old tailor was alone with his goat. Next morning he went down to her shed, patted her and said, "Come along, dear little goat, I'll take you out to graze myself." And he took her by the halter and led her to a place where there were hedges with green leaves, and yarrow, and all the other things goats like to eat. "There, now you can eat your fill for once," he told her, and he let her graze there until evening. Then he asked, "Goat, have you had enough to eat?"

And the goat replied: "I'm full up to the teeth.

Couldn't eat another leaf.

Ble-ea-eat! Ble-ea-eat!"

"Come along home, then," said the old tailor, and he led her back to her shed and tied her up. As he was leaving the shed, he turned back once more and said, "Well, at least you've had enough to eat this time!"

But the goat behaved no better to him, and she said:

"Where would I get enough to eat?

I've been jumping over stony ground,

where there wasn't a blade of grass to be found.

Ble-ea-eat! Ble-ea-eat!"

On hearing this, the tailor was taken aback, and he realized he had driven his three sons away for no good reason. "You wait, you ungrateful creature! Turning you out isn't punishment enough. I'm going to mark you so that you'll never dare show your face again in the company of honest tailors!"

He ran upstairs, fetched his razor, soaped the goat's head and shaved it as smooth as the palm of his hand. And as he thought the yardstick too good for her, he fetched his whip and beat her until she went leaping and bounding away. Now that the tailor was all alone in his house, he began to feel very sad, and wished his sons were home again, but no one knew where they had gone.

The eldest had apprenticed himself to a joiner. He was industrious and hard-working, and when his apprenticeship was over and it was time for him to go on his travels his master gave him a little table. It didn't look very grand, and it was made of ordinary wood, but it had one very fine quality. When you set it down and said, "Little table, lay yourself," all of a sudden that good little table would be laid with a clean cloth and a plate, a knife, fork, and spoon beside the plate, and dishes of meat both roast and boiled, as many as the table would hold, and a great big glass of red wine shining fit to gladden your heart.

"Well," thought the young journeyman joiner, "here's something that will last me all my life!" And he went off on his travels, merry and cheerful, and never minded whether an inn was good or bad, or whether he could get a good meal there. If he didn't feel like it, he wouldn't go to an inn at all, but would take his little table off his back and put it down in a field or wood or meadow, anywhere he liked, saying, "Little table, lay yourself," and then he had everything his heart could wish for.

At last he thought to himself that he would like to go back to his father, whose anger would have died down by now, and who would be glad to take him in again with the little table that laid itself.

It so happened that on his way home, when evening came, he went into an inn full of people. The other guests welcomed him, and invited him to sit down and share their meal, saying that otherwise he wasn't likely to get anything to eat. "No, thank you," said the joiner. "I won't take the bread out of your mouths – you must all be my guests instead."

They laughed, thinking he was joking with them. But he put his little wooden table down in the middle of the room and said, "Little table, lay yourself!" In a moment it was covered with food better than any the landlord of the inn could have served up, and the smell of it rose deliciously to the guests' nostrils.

"Help yourselves, friends," said the joiner, and when the guests saw he meant it, they took out their knives and started eating heartily. What surprised them most of all was that when a dish was empty, a full one appeared in its place all of its own accord.

The landlord stood in a corner, watching. He didn't know what to make of it, but he thought: I could do with a cook like that in my inn.

The joiner and his companions made merry till late into the night. At last they lay down to sleep, and the young journeyman went to bed too and put his wishing table by the wall. However, the landlord's thoughts would give him no peace, and it occurred to him that he had a little old table which looked just the same in his lumber room. He quietly went and fetched it, and exchanged it for the wishing table.

Next morning the joiner paid for his night's lodging, put his little table on his back with never a suspicion that it wasn't the right one, and went his way. At mid-day he came to his father's, and the tailor welcomed him joyfully.

"Well, dear son, and what have you learned?" the tailor asked him.

"I've learned to be a joiner, Father."

"That's a good trade," replied the old man, "and what have you brought back from your travels?"

"The best thing I've brought back is this little table, Father."

The tailor looked it over and said, "Well, that's nothing special. It's just an ordinary little old table."

"Ah, but it's a table that lays itself," replied his son. "If I put it down and say, 'Little table, lay yourself,' it's instantly covered with the finest of dishes, and wine to gladden your heart. So ask all our friends and relations along and we'll give them a real feast, for the table will feed them all."

When the guests had all arrived, he put his table down in the middle of the room and said, "Little table, lay yourself." But the table didn't move, and was still as empty as any other table that doesn't understand human speech.

So then the poor journeyman realized that his table had been exchanged for another, and he felt ashamed to stand there looking like a liar. As for his relations, they laughed at him, and had to go home again without food or drink. The father went back to his tailoring, and the son went off to work as a master joiner.

The second son had apprenticed himself to a miller. When he had served his apprentice-ship, the master miller said, "You've done so well that I'm giving you a donkey of a very special kind. He doesn't pull a cart, nor yet carry sacks."

"Then what's he good for?" asked the young journeyman.

"He spits gold," replied the miller. "If you stand him on a cloth and say 'Bricklebrit,' this excellent donkey will spit you gold from his mouth and drop it from his backside."

"What a fine thing!" said the journeyman, and he thanked his master and went out into the world. When he needed money, he had only to say "Bricklebrit" to his donkey to get a shower of gold pieces, and all he had to do was put himself to the trouble of picking them up. Wherever he went, only the best was good enough for him, and the more it cost the better, since his purse was always full.

When he had been on his travels for a while, seeing something of the world, he thought: I ought to go and see my father; if I come home with my gold donkey, he'll forget his anger and take me in.

Now it so happened that he came to the same inn where his brother's table had been exchanged for another. He was leading his donkey, and the landlord was about to take the animal from him and tie it up, but the young journeyman said, "Don't trouble. I'll take my Neddy here to the stable and tie him up myself, for I need to know where he is."

This seemed strange to the landlord, and he thought that a man who had to look after his own donkey wouldn't have much money to spend.

But when the stranger put his hand in his pocket, brought out two gold pieces and told him to go and buy him something really good, he stared in surprise, went out and bought the very best he could find.

After supper the guest asked what he owed. The landlord decided to charge twice the proper price, and said he must pay another two gold pieces. The journeyman put his hand in his pocket, but found he had run out of gold. "Wait a moment, landlord," said he. "I'll just go and get some more." And off he went, taking the tablecloth with him. The landlord couldn't think why. Feeling curious, he followed quietly, and since his guest bolted the stable door, he looked through a knothole.

The stranger spread the cloth underneath the donkey, said "Bricklebrit!" and next moment the animal began disgorging gold from both ends, so that it was positively raining gold on the ground. "My word!" said the landlord. "That's a good quick way to mint money! I could do with a purse like that!" The guest paid what he owed, and lay down to sleep, but in the night the landlord went down to the stable, led the donkey that would mint money away, and tied up another donkey in his place.

Early next morning the journeyman miller set off with the animal, thinking it was his own gold donkey. At mid-day he reached his father's house. The tailor was glad to see him again, and welcomed him home.

"And what's become of you, my son?" asked the old man.

"I'm a miller, dear Father," said he.

"What have you brought back from your travels?"

"Oh, only a donkey."

"There are plenty of donkeys here," said his father. "I'd rather have had a good goat."

"Ah," said his son, "but this is no ordinary donkey. It's a gold donkey. When I say, 'Bricklebrit!' the good creature disgorges enough gold to cover a cloth. So ask all our relations along and I'll make them rich."

"That's not a bad idea," said the tailor. "I wouldn't need to toil away with my needle any more then." And he went off himself to summon all their relations. As soon as they had all arrived, the miller told them to stand back, spread his cloth on the floor and brought the donkey into the room. "Now, watch this!" said he, and he cried, "Bricklebrit!" But it wasn't gold pieces the donkey dropped, and you could see the animal knew nothing of the art of making gold. Well, not every donkey can do it. Then the poor miller looked very glum, realizing he'd been cheated, and he apologized to his relations, who went home as poor as they had come. There was nothing one could do about it: the old man had to turn to his needle again, and his son went out to work for a miller.

The third brother had apprenticed himself to a turner, and as turning with the lathe is skilled work, his apprenticeship was the longest. However, his brothers wrote him a letter, telling him about their misfortunes, and how the landlord had cheated them out of their fine magic possessions. When the turner had finished his apprenticeship and was to go on his travels, his master gave him a sack for working so well, and said, "There's a cudgel inside."

"I can put the sack on my back," said the turner, "and it'll come in handy, but what's the use of the cudgel inside it? It will only weigh the sack down."

"I'll tell you what use it is," said his master. "If anyone ever does you harm, just say, 'Out of the sack cudgel!' and the cudgel will jump out among such people and beat them on the back so hard they won't be able to move for a week, nor will it stop until you say, 'Back in the sack, cudgel!'"

The journeyman thanked him, put the sack on his back, and when anyone meant to do him harm, he would say, "Out of the sack, cudgel!" and at once the cudgel would jump out among such people and beat their backs right through their coats or jackets. Well, in the evening the young turner came to the inn where his brothers had been cheated. He put his bag down on the table in front of him, and began to talk about all the wonders he had seen in the world. "Yes," said he, "you may find a table that lays itself, a donkey that spits gold and so forth, and very good things they are too, I don't deny it. But that's all nothing to the treasure I've got, that I carry around with me in my sack there."

The landlord pricked up his ears, and wondered what in the world it could be. "The sack must be filled with jewels", he thought, "and I ought to get my hands on them." When it was time to go to sleep, the young man lay down and put his sack under his head for a pillow. Once the landlord thought his guest was fast asleep, he went and tugged very gently at the sack, to see if he could get it out from under the young man's head and put another in its place. But that was what the turner had been waiting for all this time. And just as the landlord was about to give a good jerk, he cried, "Out of the sack, cudgel!" The cudgel instantly came out of the sack, made for the landlord and beat him black and blue.

The landlord howled for mercy, but the louder he howled, the harder the cudgel beat his back in time to his yells, until at last he fell to the ground exhausted. Then the turner said, "If you don't give me back the table that lays itself and the gold donkey, we'll start the dance again."

"No, no," cried the landlord, very crestfallen now, "I'll be glad to give them both back, only make that wretched imp go into the sack again!"

"I'll go easy on you this time," said the journeyman, "but mind what may happen to you!" And he cried, "Into the sack, cudgel!" and gave it a rest.

Next morning the turner went home to his father with the table that laid itself and the gold donkey. The tailor was glad to see him back, and asked him too what he had learned while he was away.

"I'm a turner, dear Father," said he.

"That's a skilled trade," said his father. "And what have you brought back from your travels?"

"Something precious, dear Father," replied his son. "A cudgel in a sack."

"What?" cried his father. "A cudgel! Why, that's not worth a thing. You can cut a cudgel from any tree."

"Not one like this, dear Father. If I say, 'Out of the sack, cudgel!' the cudgel jumps out and leads anyone who means to harm me a merry dance, and it won't leave off until he's down on the ground and begging for mercy. Look — with the aid of this cudgel, I got back the table that lays itself and the gold donkey that the thieving landlord stole from my brothers. So send for them both, and ask our relations along, and I'll give them food and drink and fill their pockets with gold."

The old tailor wasn't sure whether to believe this, but he asked all their relations along. Then the turner spread a cloth on the floor of the room, led the gold donkey in and told his brother, "Now, dear brother, speak to him."

"Bricklebrit!" said the miller, and at once gold pieces showered down on the cloth like a downpour of rain, and the donkey didn't stop until they all had so much gold they couldn't carry any more. (And I can tell you'd have liked to be there too.)

Then the turner fetched the little table and said, "Dear brother, speak to it now."

And no sooner had the joiner said, "Little table, lay yourself!" than it was laid, and covered with the finest of dishes. Then there was such a banquet as the good tailor had never had in his house before, and all their relations stayed on making merry until late into the night. The tailor put his needle and thread, yardstick and smoothing iron away in a cupboard, and lived in luxury with his three sons.

But what became of the goat? Well, I'll tell you. She was ashamed of her shaven head, so she went into a fox's hole and hid there. When the fox came home, he saw a pair of big eyes glowing at him in the dark, and he was afraid and ran away again. The bear met him, and seeing the fox looking so upset, he asked, "What's the matter, Brother Fox? Why do you look like that?" "Oh," said Reynard Fox, "there's a terrible animal in my home, and it stared at me with its fiery eyes."

"We'll soon drive it out," said the bear, and he went back to the fox's hole with him and looked in. However, when he saw the fiery eyes, he was frightened too, and ran away. The bee met him, and seeing that he seemed most uneasy, she said, "You look very grumpy, bear. Where's your usual good temper?"

"It's all very well for you to talk," said the bear, "but there's a fierce animal with staring eyes in Reynard Fox's hole, and we can't get it out again."

"Well, I feel sorry for you, bear," said the bee. "I'm a poor, feeble creature, and the pair of you wouldn't so much as look at me in the usual way, but still I think I can help you." So she flew into the fox's hole, sat on the goat's smooth, shorn head, and stung it so hard that the goat jumped up, bleating, ran away like a mad thing, and to this day nobody knows where she went.